LOVE-
A Million Shades

NISHKA DHAWAN

PARTRIDGE
A Penguin Random House Company

To order additional copies of this book, contact
Partridge India
000 800 10062 62
www.partridgepublishing.com/india
orders.india@partridgepublishing.com

Break me baby now isn't that easy
Kill me baby, don't let me breathe
Hurt me baby be my worst nightmare
But in the end,
Kiss me baby like the world's ending . . .

Contents

SECTION 1

In love:

SECTION 2

Broken:

Falling apart:

Barely Breathing:

SECTION 3

Hell:

Reincarnation:

SHORT STORIES

SECTION 1

In love:

I love you without knowing how, or when, or from where. I love you simply, without problems or pride: I love you in this way because I do not know any other way of loving but this, in which there is no I or you, so intimate that your hand upon my chest is my hand, so intimate that when I fall asleep your eyes close.

Pablo Neruda

A love letter.

Take my hand, cross the river.
Nothing matters when you're with me.
The sun shines brighter, the water looks clearer.
The worlds a better place when you're with me.
Sorrows don't exist, because when I'm with you
Baby you take it all away.
So come with me across this river,
I'll be you guide, you're guardian angel.
Your love forever.
The worlds too big to be alone,
I need you to hold my hand.
We'll make our own little place
In this vast land.
The mountains will seem small,
The ocean a glass of water.
Because baby when I'm with you
No obstacle ever matters.
In sickness or in health,
For rich or for poor,
In happiness or in sadness
We will be together, forever.
So come with me across this river,
In to our world. Where we will live together.
In darkness or in light, in life or in death,
We are bound forever.

Across the stars.

The sky's our home,
We travel across the galaxy
Hand in hand.
It's a perfect place, it's our home
The stars wink at us
As we travel across dimensions,
Hand in hand.
Our love shining brighter than all of them.

His eyes

Those eyes, rare striking manipulative,
They stand out in a crowd.
Those dark eyes so different than the ones around them,
Giving away his demeanor so easily.
Those sparkling eyes, his arrogance
So riveting, grounding me to the spot.
But they aren't looking into mine.
His dark eyes, one shade of black
Masking his many moods.
I see them so clearly
His eyes like a mirror.
I will him to look at me.
And then he does.
Everything changes.
I feel his pull.
My feet guiding me to him.
Nothing else matters now,
He's captured me.
They found mine . . .

Greece

It was a cold day.
I shivered even under the suns rays.
People all around me were smiling and beaming.
Yet I was so lost.
In the land of the past.
The view was breathtaking. A different world
So far away from reality, so enchanting.
Yet I felt so lost.
And then I saw him.
His six foot frame blocked the sun.
The rays playing a game with his golden brown hair.
His eyes, were the shade of coffee in the morning
And they were looking at me.
His beige tee clung to his physique.
The wind slowly brushing his hair
And in the land of Greece
He was a god so fierce and fair.
His lips tilted up to reveal a small smile
And I was enraptured by his beauty
So caught up in him that I couldn't hear anything.
Until I was snapped out of my trance.
I turned around to see who was beckoning me
And when I looked back he was gone.
Just like that I was lost again . . .

Don't be a stranger

Don't stand there like you don't know me,
Don't pretend you don't see me.
You know I'm here,
So don't push me away when I get near.
You say you don't need me,
But you do baby,
I see it.
So don't be a stranger.
Come close, hold me tight,
Trust when I say things will be all right
Cause baby I won't let anything happen to you,
I'll hold you close,
Wipe those tears away,
I'll say all the right things,
Cause baby I love you so.
So come close, hold me tight.
Baby don't be a stranger to me

Nishka Dhawan

Do you love me?

The room is bathed in rose petals.
A violinist playing a soft tune.
All around me there's pictures
Of me with him.
And then he enters,
Holding the biggest bouquet of lilacs I've ever seen
He comes up to me, his face bathed in love.
"When a man gives a women a lilac,
He's asking her a question."
I look in to his sincere eyes, awaiting my response.
It takes me a heartbeat to reply,
And it's what he wants to hear.

Three lives one feeling.

Sunshine bathes my room
It is a new day
I breathe in the fresh morning air.
It's so beautiful
A new day has come to life
Giving us a chance to dream,
Spread our wings.
It's so beautiful.
I step out of my reverie
And I see him.
Everything changes.
He is so beautiful.

Smiles beam all around me,
My newfound success noted by everyone
Surrounded by a sea of people
All believing in me
It's the best feeling ever,
Being on top of the world forever
I've never wanted to be so alive
My ambition making me strive.
Tears of joy and greetings
Flowers, loved ones and meetings.
I never thought this day could get more perfect
Until I saw him.

It is a boring meeting.
Insistent chatter in closing a deal.
I run a hand through my hair in frustration.
"No more no less." That's my deal.
More chatter, now I'm starting to lose it.
"Take it or leave it"
How much longer?
God this is frustrating.
The door knocks
And she walks in.
"Sorry for the delay"
I sit stunned.
Who is this breathtaking beauty?
"The deals off" She curtly says
And everything changes.
Cause of her.

Untitled

Stars fall from the sky,
Dashing hope,
Searing deep through my soul.
Crashing stars, blinding sight,
Exuding darkness, agony, fright.
Stand alone, no light
But bright eyes watching,
Winking, twinkling.
Crash!
They rain down from above,
Around me.
Thick shards of heat, light, flame
Bathing me in fiery rain,
Showering me with a bright blaze,
Lighting me up from within, so harsh
Radiating into the night,
Fiery light,
The love of my life.

Nishka Dhawan

Dying hope

For years this rose I tended upon,
But today, it's first petal I see gone . . .
Disheartened and torn my rose I looked upon,
Astounded to see it's beauty all gone . . .

It's scarlet blush began to fade,
It's verdant arms no more swayed.
It's pink hue began turning grey,
All it needed was a sun's ray . . .

But merciless was the sun,
Warmth it gave none,
Left my rose to shrivel and die,
Watching it wilt, tears filled my eyes . . .

I raised my hand to savor it's dew,
As a cool wind over me blew,
I stopped my hand mid-air,
As another petal from my dear rose began to tear . . .

I could watch it's pain no more,
My hands and feet began to turn sore,
I prayed to god to save my rose,
Weeping, crying holding it close.

My roses' misery I could feel,
It's grief I wanted to heal,
But there I was helpless,
And it's pain I was unable to suppress . . .

The slight chill turned into a mighty storm,
I embraced my rose trying to keep it warm,
But the universe was conspiring against us,
So I came close and kissed my rose thus,
And watched the end approach us . . .

I stayed embracing my rose motionless,
Until the storm slowly began to repress,
I gradually lifted my head to gaze upon what was left of my
rose,
Seeing it perish, my body froze . . .

As my rose took in it's last breath,
I watched it approach it's death . . .
Wretched and inconsolable my eyes once again filled with
tears,
I remembered the happy memories we spent over the years . . .

Free

A cage so strong holding me captive,
Flapping my wings, wanting to be free.
Struggling to just be alive.
Each day I see the day fade to night
And see them fly past me and I miss it.
He visits my cage every evening secretly,
Always hoping one day he'll find it open
But our love is so forbidden,
That if master found out, I'd be hidden.
I yearn to be free with him,
Live my life in the beauty of the sky
Yet I can only feel freedom through his eyes
While he feels pain through mine.
One day I will be free,
One day we would be together
And till then I can only hope.

Moments

How fast can your life change?
One year
You meet someone who changes your past.
One month
You grow older, you run away from your past
One day
Time vanishes; you can't remember your past
One minute
You realize you're dictating your past
One second
You remember you are the past . . .

First day to work.

The alarm sets off awaking me from my deep slumber. I was dreaming of dead dark eyes, eyes that I couldn't quite place. Oh well, it was probably just my hangover getting the better of me. I lay back down trying to catch another two minutes of sleep before I had to get ready for my first day of work. I had just graduated from business school in Wichita, Kansas and now I was in New York, the city that never sleeps. It's going to take some getting used to. The first time I stepped into the New York air, it was sensory overload. The honking of taxis, loud pedestrians, feeling of the metro under my feet was all new. It felt like a whole different country and I stared dumbstruck and wide-eyed at the wonder and bright lights of the city.

Getting off the bed, I took a quick shower and slipped on one of my pencil skirts and paired it up with a white silk top. Carefully pulling up my brown hair in an elegant bun, slipping on some lip-gloss and pinching my cheeks to get some color I passed myself as presentable. It was around seven thirty and I had exactly half an hour to get to my new job. I left my Brooklyn apartment waving at the doorman on my way out. My mother was a practitioner and one of the most respected neurosurgeons in the states. It was a shock to her when I told her my interest lied in business and not science. Her dream had always been to see me become a heart surgeon, but my persistence won out in the end and she supported me in my dreams. My first job is that of a junior assistant to the company's owner, Mr. Van Crest. I never got to meet him though. The senior assistant had guided me through my interview. He was easy to talk to with kind brown eyes that offset his pale freckled face. I immediately connected with him and was happy to know he would be the one I'd normally report to. After a brief ten-minute walk I approached the massive building, Lyrambrosia. As beautiful as it was on the outside with its glass windows all the way to the top story completed with a helipad, it was even better on the interior.

A gush of cool breeze greeted me as I entered through the revolving doors. All around me people brisk walked dressed in immaculate suits or sheathed dresses. I flashed my Id card at the reception and was just in time to get in to the elevators. It was crowded in there. Serious faces all around me where engrossed in the tiny screens of cell phones in front of them. Many of them cast furtive glances my way but when the elevator doors opened it was all lost in a frenzy of scurrying out the double doors and in to the plush lobby. I greeted the receptionist while she returned my warm greeting with a tight smile. It seemed like I was the only one to greet her. I tried not to notice too much how everyone treated me like an outsider and headed to report to the senior assistant, Sean Wilson.

With two knocks I entered the room to find him in deep conversation with another man. Even with his back faced to me this man exuded power and confidence. Power leeched out of him casting a ghostly embrace all around him. I was so latched on to his figure that I didn't realize when Sean greeted me. "Helix? Miss Bedloe?" he repeated. 'Huh? Uhh . . . sorry sir." I said embarrassed. At this uncharacteristic greeting *he* turned around. His gaze bore in to mine and I stared back dumbstruck. He had those eyes . . . the ones that haunted me every night. It fixed me to the spot; I couldn't blink, move or say a word. I was immobilized. Sean stepped forward, oblivious to the tension in the room and began introductions. "Helix meet the owner of Van Crest enterprises and holdings, Mr. Tyran Van Crest." Then directing his attention to Tyran he said, " Mr. Crest, this is the new junior assistant Miss Helix Bedloe." He was still holding my gaze, unblinking. His attention towards me made me shudder. He probably noticed that as a second later a wicked smile played across his perfectly sculpted lips. I imagined those lips all over me and couldn't help but let a faint blush creep all over my face. He stepped forward offering me a hand and then in a low, husky voice he said, "Nice meeting you Helix, I look forward to working with you," and then softy so that only I could hear he continued, "To our next, hopefully private meeting." That line definitely made me go scarlet; I could feel the heat move across my skin or maybe, it was the heat emanating from his lean powerful body. Not knowing how else to respond I offered him a small smile and placed my hand in his. The physical connection caught me off guard. His touch jolted throughout my body making every nerve ending sing. He had hardly touched me and I was already turned on. He made me feel exposed, vulnerable. He shook my hand lightly and released it. I was startled at how disappointed I felt. What was wrong with me? He's my boss for Christ's sake. I needed some air. I excused myself from the two gentlemen and told Sean I would be in my cubicle when he was done with Mr. Van Crest. With that said I made a hasty exit, and entered my tiny cubicle a few steps away and put my head in my hands, thinking about the unusual encounter I just had with Mr. 'I control you". Who the hell was he? But one thing was damn clear, whoever he was, he had trouble written all over him.

A discovery.

The blaring of horns spun me back to reality. The hard gravel raked against my skin, while I struggled to procure a single breath. All of a sudden, the ground blurred again, passerby's voices muffled together in a chaotic rumble and my head felt light. The last thing I recalled was being lifted up in to his arms and then . . . I blacked out.

My eyes fluttered open to focus on the tear stained face of my mother. I'd never seen her so broken over something since my father's death. I guess I really did look like hell right now.

"Honey", she croaked, new tears running down the path of her old ones. "Honey, how are you feeling?" she continued concerned.

"Mom, I'm fine", I managed to answer past my closed throat.

"I'm so sorry, if I . . . if you, if you hadn't seen what you did, you wouldn't have left . . ." She trailed off.

"It doesn't matter, I don't blame you . . . I should've let you explain . . . I'm sorry I didn't."

"Oh honey, come here", she said, gingerly embracing my limp body. A dozen questions were clouding my hand. What had I seen her doing? I remembered the circle connected with the ends of a glowing star. I remembered her clad in a black robe, muttering a chant in a foreign language. I remember all their faces; pale as marble, while her eyes were onyx and not the cerulean blue I was accustomed to seeing. It terrified me so much that I darted from the door, just to be hit by an ongoing car on the crowded streets of Manhattan. The world that I had seen inside my home was a huge contrast to the vibrant New York City. The darkness when I walked in was enough to prove that something was not quite right. When I had walked further in to the apartment, following the hushed tone of chanting, the cabs, horns, screaming, everything tuned out. I felt as though I had entered another universe, and my mom had to explain to me what on earth was she doing.

A soft knock on the door snapped me back to reality. A head of a young guy peeked in to my desolate room. "May I speak with her", he asked addressing my mother. My mother looked doubtful, crease marks forming across her forehead while she tried to come up with a reason to shoo him away. Before she could utter a word I said, "hey . . ." He entered the room before replying, "hey." I looked towards my mother hoping she would get the sign to give me some privacy. She either didn't care or feigned ignorance. I looked sternly at her before saying, "Mom, would you mind checking with the doctor to see if all the paper work is signed?" "I can do that later honey," she said, not at all happy with the tone I used on her. "If you don't mind, I'd like it if you did it now," I said with all my resolve. "fine', she said tightlipped before stiffly walking out the room.

I didn't know what to say, so we stayed silent for a few moments, just looking at each other, the only sound coming from the steady beep on the heart monitor. He was beautiful. His dark hair framed the olive skin of his face attractively, enhancing his sculpted lips and aristocratic nose greatly. His eyes were not just any blue, but the exact shade of sapphire, and those gorgeous eyes were focused on me. I couldn't do anything but helplessly look back at them.

He broke the silence a few moments later. "That was a pretty nasty hit you took huh," he said, his mouth curving up to one side to reveal a dimple. He walked a few steps and sat beside me on the bed. Up close I noticed how lush and long his eyelashes were. God, he looked like a Greek god come to life. As he set his arm on the other side of my hospital bed, I noticed something on the inside of his wrist. It looked like a tattoo of sorts, with an eye branching out to meet his veins. It looked diabolical, but then again, I never quite got a good look at it since he placed his arm right on his lap the moment I took interest in his tattoo. " I guess", I said trying to smile but wincing instead. "Thank you for helping me, I . . . I owe you my life." I continued. "You don't owe me anything Sophie, I'm just glad you're ok." The sincere look in his eyes was overwhelming. It seemed like he really cared bout me, but that seemed impossible since we hadn't even officially been introduced. Then it clicked me. "How do you know my name", I asked, my tone creeping towards the interrogative edge. "I took the liberty of checking the name of the girl I saved.", he answered, matter-of-factly. I eased a little satisfied with his answer. My day had been such a mess that I couldn't even trust the guy who saved my life. Trying to lighten things up I said, "You never told me you name, I should know the name of the guy who saved my life right?" Just then my mom barged through the door. He saw this as a cue to leave. Just before he walked out the door he said "its Gabe, my name."

SECTION 2

Broken:

"The heart was made to be broken."

Oscar Wilde

How much I miss you

I see you there, but you're not the same.
Your eyes act like they don't know me.
And when I try to reach out to you,
You act like you don't care.
Don't you remember those times?
When we'd start and end our days together,
But now I'd be lucky to hear from you at all.
What happened to us?
Why when I look at you,
I see someone else.
All I think is the guy I knew is dead.
But how can you move on
When I keep believing that you're there
Somewhere . . . Inside that guy
That looks like you . . .
I'm begging you to be him again.
The one I knew.
Because I cant live like this.
I want you back.

You just had to break me

It painful to believe that you hurt me
When I trusted you with my life.
You took my love for granted
And tore me apart on the inside.
My scars gushing red, un-healing,
My past a hurdle, still dealing.
And now you came,
Flipped my world around
And destroyed my life so easy,
Wasn't it enough to see me hurting?
But you still had to do it further,
Again and again torture me,
Destroy me,
Kill me . . .

Untitled 2

He asks me to trust him,
Tell him what goes through my mind
But the he says things,
Does things,
That hurt me so deep
Flooding me with despair
Making me regret knowing him.
Nothing matters then.
Life feels empty
Happiness washes away
There's nothing left for me
But an empty hollowness
That lasts forever.
It consumes me,
Burns me,
Scars me,
Takes away my soul.
It leaves me empty.
He leaves me empty.

Nishka Dhawan

What is life?

I desire to write but words don't form,
I need the cold but yearn for warmth,
I know the truth but I live in a lie,
what is life, when anytime one can die.
I think about the future when I can't accept my past,
I'm always first, yet I finish last,
I wish it would rain on a sunny day,
I can't speak, when I know what to say.
I think i'm wrong when others say i'm right,
What is life, when nowhere I can see light.
I hate the people I love,
I look below instead of above,
I act first think later,
What is life, when everyone thinks i'm a hater.
Oh tell me why this is so,
Whats wrong with me I don't even know,
Oh what is life when everyone is against me,
Oh what is life if nothing but cruelty . . .

Numb

Drag drag drag,
One more step,
One more tear,
One more day.
Fear turns against me,
Making me numb,
Numb to everything around me,
Except for him.
My heart beats twice as fast,
My body shudders, trembles,
Nails dig into my palms,
I can't take another step,
So I fall, but I don't feel anything,
Because I'm numb . . .

Love—In reality

Love, Oh love it poisons your heart,
Love, Oh love makes your whole world fall apart.
It imbues and captivates your body and soul,
And ravages your being as a whole.
By dashing through your blood and veins,
It ensnares you and creates its own private hurricane
Where your emotions are wrapped up in a tumult,
Leaving you baffled and flustered as a result.
You bruise and scar in this battle of wills,
Where love leads, as it thrills and kills.
Struggling and tackling whatever comes your way,
You still lose this skirmish to your dismay.
Exposed and defenseless love takes you over,
As you wail and snivel while you cower

Real life

painted a picture across the sky,
A prince, a princess, a palace . . .
A perfect love story.
One we all dream off.
But what happens next?
After the happily ever after.
I want to believe in never-ending love.
I want to believe in forever after's
But he never lets me.
So my painted picture is not reality,
It's my imagination.
I want it to happen
But it never will.

Nishka Dhawan

Waiting

It was a beautiful day,
I was so happy,
My love was coming to me.
I spent the day primping myself,
Waiting for him to appear.
He should have been here by now.
But he did not turn up.
I had to wait.
And I waited for three more hours.
The clips in my hair were undone,
My make up was fading.
He still wasn't here.
I let myself drift off
When a door bell rang
Awakening my slumber.
I opened the door
But it wasn't him.
It was the police.
And they were holding his engagement ring,
The one I gave him.
The ring had bloodstains on it.
And I knew
It was the end, I could feel it.
He was gone . . .

Cry

My eyes welled up with tears,
All at once I was faced with my deepest sorrows and fears.
My muscles strained and I started breathing hard,
When I found out from his memory me he had jarred.
I couldn't endure the agony anymore,
So I broke down and let my anguish pour.
Letting the tears stream down my face,
I couldn't fathom why from his memory me he resolved to erase.
Knowing he loved me no more my heart burned,
My body and soul for him yearned,
Clutching my heart I realized our connection was gone,
I knew he had already moved on.
I was deluding myself thinking he could ever belong to me
Or letting myself believe that he loved me madly,
I realized that I had to let him go,
My heart drowned in an ocean of woe,
So I sat steady embracing my knees,
Trying to put my mind at ease,
But the intensity of my feelings I failed to control
And the tears ran down my face devouring my soul . . .

There never was an 'us'

It was very simple to believe,
That you and me had something together.
But now I know the truth,
Realization struck me hard
When I heard it out loud,
That you're not interested in me
That everything we had was a lie.
You and me were nothing
Just two strangers
Whose paths crossed for a while
And now you walked away,
Leaving me standing
And realization struck me hard.
I am just a stranger to you

Love kills

It's crazy being the victim of love,
The pain a whole new degree,
People who you thought you could trust,
Corrode you with their lies, make you rust.
I'm fading now with all their broken promises,
My face now paling, eyes watering.
I never thought I deserved this
But life obviously had other plans for me.
It's not easy being alone,
Accepting that you have no one
Happiness, joy, you have none.
But I have no choice but to try to move on,
Completely fade away, be gone
Because when you're hurt as bad as me
There's no way out
Just your sorrow as deep as the sea.
All I do is focus on the highlights
But even that isn't easy
For now I see the devil in their faces
Those words they said now sound evil, cruel
That's what they did to me
They broke me,
Shattered me,
Killed me.

Nishka Dhawan

The girl in the mirror

The mirror stares back at you.
Who is she?
A shadow at best,
A miserable beast at worst.
She looks pale.
Her face anguished.
Tear drops stained with blood.
Chafed lips, swollen eyes.
Who is she?
I look at her, she doesn't speak.
Her eyes giving away her pain.
So hurtful to watch.
She's crying again.
For some reason my face feels wet.
I raise my hand to wipe my eyes
And so does she.
My eyes widen in alarm
And so do hers.
I step back and so does she.
But that's not possible!
She's not me!
I'm happy, I have him.
He's here isn't he?
I'm not alone!
I look around at the empty room.
The empty bed.
The chill I feel.
It's all coming back to me.
It's not our room anymore.
It's mine.

Falling apart:

"I'm falling apart, one part after another. Falling down on the world like snow. Half of me is already on the ground, watching from below."

— **Ashly Lorenzana**

Untitled 3

Total control is just an illusion.
We don't have power over anyone,
Just an untethered grasp which too
May never exist.
When we commit to love
We give away our strength.
We become weak.
Broken pieces of a puzzle,
Simply unsolvable.
Others take your place.
Try to control you . . .
And you let them
Because when you are deceived,
Your love wretched from you.
You only open yourself up to more suffering
And that devil who put you there,
Who took away your love
Is a fucking angel
Because that's what god does.
Good people suffer,
While the bad who deserve hell,
Survive in bliss . . .
And we so weak,
Miserable, lost and deceived
Are forced to live our lives in humiliation
Of failure . . .
Everything we believed in,
Now just a dream
Which those people and god
Ripped away from you.

Its harsher than taking your life.
Living every day, in hope
Which doesn't even exist.
Everything you are,
Stripped from you.
All that is left
Is half a human being
Clinging to the past
Not able to move on
When they are capable of so much more!
But those fucking angels
Will make sure that you
DON'T achieve happiness
And God? Why pray to someone
WHO MAKES YOU SUFFER.

Do I deserve this?

I want to run away, far away.
Start over, forget my past.
I'm sick of it.
The remorse, agony, depression.
It's unfair, cruel, harsh.
Why me?
From a billion people, why me?
Oh cruel lord, forgive my sins.
Give me a new life, a purpose.
Let me move on.
Stop punishing me.
I don't deserve it.
Why me?

Untitled 4

It's dark outside,
It's a no moon night.
The clouds are everywhere,
So there are no stars.
No streetlamps, or headlights.
Silence tenfold.
You can't hear the night owl,
The crickets, the bats.
No people, not even the wind.
This is my life.

Don't go, please?

It getting harder to breathe everyday,
Life's taken a toll,
Words don't make any sense,
My attention span is zero.
Everything's going wrong,
Where are you?
My life is a pile of mess,
It's killing me,
Why can't you guess?
No one understands me,
I need you to talk to,
Come back, where are you?
I'm broken, my feelings crushed,
My silent plea, hushed.
I need you to tell me it's okay,
I need you to start everyday.
Just looking at you is not enough,
Because looking at you kill's me,
It's killing me, why can't you see?
Please come back.
Everything hurts, my hearts broken,
My worlds without color,
I can't move on,
Don't leave me,
Please,
Please come back . . .

A lost maze.

Everything is a blur,
Concentration is now my enemy.
What has he done to me?
Nothing seems to put me at rest
I don't realize it's for the best
But the nightmares haunt me at night
I can't seem to accept what's simply right
Lets put it this way,
A path you're chosen to walk through
Theres nothing you can really do
But walk
And hope that there is light.
But when the path intensifies,
Pushes you to the very end
Where there is no one to lend,
A hand
Alone you walk, alone you sacrifice
Will living a half life suffice?
Without him, fury comes ten fold
Tears seep endlessly from my eyes,
No ones hand to hold
Or shoulder to cry on
All your happiness completely gone
But you must go on
Have that extraordinary gift of hope
That every sad story has a happy ending
That every broken heart receives tending
That life will fix itself
That justice will be served . . .

Untitled 5

Insomnia,
A continuous train of thought
With no ending.
Overthinking,
Driving you crazy,
No sense of direction,
No control.
Powerless, lost, confused.
Loss of dreams,
That one person that changed
My life.
Gone.
Missing him is all I have,
Its all I live for.

Alone forever

Trust loyalty friendship,
A soft kiss on the lip
The ghost of his embrace,
The white dress all in lace.
Time ticks and stops
Rain falls in enormous drops
The night doesn't seem to end
Oh what is there to mend.
Sorrows flow from a leaky faucet
Nothing dries the tears away . . .
The sound of joy seems too far
The memories that I cannot jar
Vows promised meant to hold on to
Now lost in a dark abyss
A forgotten string of thoughts
Before I ever met him
Now lost with his soul . . .
My heart so easily he stole
Now I live, heartless
Lost directionless
The betrayal hurts no less
While he spends his life now with her.
His love for me seems so untrue
While I ask myself the question,
What did I mean to him?
Those words he said
Did he really love me too?
But then it happened
What I most dread.
And now he's gone . . .
Evermore . . .
I will never reach the shore . . .

Dominos

One touch and the dominos fall endlessly,
Each one nudging the other,
A never-ending chain,
Like the continuous pitter-patter of the rain.
Much like life,
How one event is the result of another,
Like the far away thunder
Precedes the cloudburst.
As One by one fall the dominos,
One by one pass the days . . .

Where are you?

I see you there, but you're not the same.
Your eyes act like they don't know me.
And when I try to reach out to you,
You act like you don't care.
Don't you remember those times?
When we'd start and end our days together,
But now I'd be lucky to hear from you at all.
What happened to us?
Why when I look at you,
I see someone else.
All I think is the guy I knew is dead.
But how can I move on
When I keep believing that you're there
Somewhere . . . Inside that guy
That looks like you . . .
I'm begging you to be him again.
The one I knew.
Because I cant live like this.
I want you back.

Another day goes by . . .

Another day goes by,
Life isn't as easy as peach pie,
Everyday it seems like the worlds at end,
My wounds are bleeding, theres no way to mend.
Thou am no one to him.
Never was, never will be.
He obliterated every aspect of me,
The fact that he forgot me completely
Still seems hard to believe . . .
Six years in a row,
Can you imagine?
Look at what he's done.
Destroyed me to the vey core,
Life without him seems so sore.
No more doors exist
Paths are lost
Memories turned to dust,
A ghost grin on his handsome face
That once belonged to me
Now lost amongst the darkness
Oh how hard is it to see
What's right in front of me
Centuries of lost love now await
Immortal heart break
Lie awake me in the middle of the night
Not a singe ray of sunlight,
Lost memories of the past
Old lives, old friends
Come and go

Life won't stop
Tears wont end
I need to move on
Believe he's gone
Accept what lies in front of my eyes
Believe that all he gave me was lies
While tears filled my eyes
Now the sun will never rise
All I can do is roll a dice
To survive, to survive . . .

He took my life

I have nothing left.
He took it all away.
I don't even know what happiness is anymore.
I don't know if I'll ever be happy.
I am so in love with him
But it doesn't even matter.
He will never feel the same way about me.
No body ever will.
He took my life away
And I'm not even alive anymore.

Untitled 6

Thoughts unfurling in my mind.
That lost dream, my reverie . . .
Where did he go,
Amongst the shadows I looked for him.
A room surrounded by mirrors,
His face shining back at me.
The moon up high in the sky.
His face, lost in the shadows.
That's where I looked for him.
Dancing across the room,
Following his light.
The swish of my skirt,
Hair swaying behind me.
Stop, no voice, no face, no light.
Wind blows crashing windows,
Glass everywhere.
Mirrors shaking violently,
An explosion of glass
All around me.
My white dress now torn,
Scars covering my hands,
A black room surrounding me so quiet,
He was just a dream . . .

Barely Breathing:

"Heaven has no rage like love to hatred turned,
nor hell a fury like a woman scorned."

—**William Congreve**

Untitled 7

S ilence is the absence of words,
    Not believing what you just heard
    When reason fails you,
Conscience betrays you,
Who can you trust?
When A mindless game,
Is Played through lies,
Watching the end,
Before your very eyes.
Thoughts tumble and twist,
Cries go unheard
Screaming, banging behind the barred door.
The tinkling of bells,
Stars in the sky,
Scent of roses,
Lost . . .
The loss of you,
Echoes, loud and clear.
Long nights,
Restless dreams,
Waking up at 3 am,
Consumed by the thoughts of you . . .
Reality,
A clear sense of loss,
Loss of you

How much it hurts

The pain that hits me,
It's unbearable.
Wave after wave of turmoil
Destroying me from the inside.
I try to keep a straight face,
My facade hiding my true emotions
But sometimes it hurts so much
The pain intensified tenfold
That it gets harder to breath
And I cant live like this
Because I'm dying on the inside
And this pain, it's destroying me

Isolation

The sun pierces my eyes, ahead of me nothing lies,
My eyes rummage for a drop of water,
I loose all will to seek what I was after.
I take another step and fall to my knees,
Is this some payment for my past deeds?
I look down intently at the fine gold sand,
How far it runs covering every inch of land
My skin burns as the sun caresses my frame
I realize that life will never be the same
For what I did was unforgivable and wrong,
I let myself be weak when the time came to be strong,
So now I lie torn, and kissed by death,
As I struggle to procure another lump of breath . . .

Untitled 8

Hope.
Try and try, shut your eyes,
Hide the world.
Hush . . . .
Quietness descends,
Oblivion.
Noises cloud your sleep,
Restless, tired, agonized.
Lost love, lost dreams,
Failure. Being a failure.
Yet try,
Try and try,
But nothing changes.
No hope, nothing left.
Shhh . . .
Broken whispers,
Lost conversations,
All hushed, even you.

The sadist

The searing pain hit my core
The world turned to an unnatural blur,
His wicked laugh echoed in my ears,
As once again the jagged edge through my skin tore.
The blood dripped endlessly, clouding my vision,
And for a moment the reality faded away
Old memories caught me in a whirlwind
As I saw me happy with him.
Who would have ever placed the most eligible bachelor in town
To be the master of cruelty deep down . . .
A hard blow against my skull brought me back to my
fading senses,
As I faintly made out his sadistic face,
Once which I associated with poise and grace.
The first time I saw him, I was enraptured by his beauty
His enchanting gold eyes that caught me off guard,
His sincere smile which threw me off my feet.
I was in love I thought then
But I hadn't known better,
To him, I never really mattered.
He hid his sadist side so well,
I thought he'd love and cherish me till the end.
So when he got down on one knee,
The light shining in his diabolical eyes,
I mistook his emotions for love,
And said yes . . .
The everything turned around.
We got married the next day,
In a quaint English church,

I'd never been happier.
It all changed that night,
I finally saw his true side.
He whipped me for the first time,
And once he had the taste, he never stopped.
Reality came back harsh as
He hit me again.
The pain echoing in my back this time,
And then again, and again.
The pain ripping through my senses,
Till all I can feel is peace,
On the other side of life . . .

Untitled 9

Racing through my mind
Confusion. Tears clouding my eyes.
Heart pumping fast,
Don't know where to look,
Where to go.
Faces everywhere, but not his.
Pushing shoving, crying.
He's not here.
Now I'm tired, so lost.
Where is he?
White cloth, black suit.
Tick tock Tick tock.
No words, hushed silence.
There he is.
Lying dead.

Don't do this to me

Questions befuddle my mind,
Feelings cloud my soul,
What I don't understand though,
Is how can you be so cold?
To you, I'm the 'other' girl,
The one you hardly care about,
The one you hardly treat right,
The one you push away
With all your might.
I know I'm her,
You've made that much clear,
Yet I wish I wasn't,
For you are not the 'other' guy to me.
I let you see the real me,
The sensitive version that I hide from the world.
I let you heal me when I'm broken,
I let you talk to me when I'm shaken.
You own that piece of me,
That I try so hard to disguise,
But you obviously don't understand,
How hard it is to be what I am,
Especially when I'm with you.
I behave differently,
I treat you differently,
And you take it all for granted,
You make me wish for things I never wanted.
Your mood wears off on me,
And so I do things I'm not supposed to.
I give away my power at times,

To guys other than you.
You make me weak,
Not just with you but with everyone else.
You don't let me have peaceful dreams,
Or a nights rest,
You let me cry away at best,
You've destroyed me,
You've made me let down my walls
You've made me wish that love didn't exist . . .

Lost

My compass rotates endlessly,
My mind spins carelessly,
I keep looking for my treasure,
Been searching forever.
I crave to see its familiar face,
wrap myself in it's warm embrace,
Live a life of pleasure,
Leave it's side never,
But how do I find,
With no hope in my mind,
His mesmerizing eyes
A forgotten prize.

A shadow in the dark

I toppled over landing on my knees,
My hand laying flat over my heart,
My body quivering, experiencing unease,
All my defenses plummeting and falling apart.

I staggered to take in another wisp of air.
My breathing was haggard and strained.
Feeling the prickling of my hair,
I realized my body was imbrued and chained.

Amongst the plunging darkness,
I faintly saw his shadow appear.
I was run over by a feeling of bleakness,
My blood began brewing with fear.

His eyes, burning with fearsome cruelty,
His mouth revealing a wicked grin,
His attire, filthy and musty,
Preparing to commit a sinister sin.

I began trembling with despair,
And my legs struggled to move me back,
I fore saw the agony I was about to bear,
And braced myself for the vicious attack.

I heard him approach slow and steady,
As I noticed a whip in his hand,
For the affliction and misery I was ready,
Knowing this torture I wouldn't withstand.

He paced ahead and stood before me,
The whip swaying high above his head,
He grinned once more at me wickedly,
As from my eyes, tears began to shed.

He lashed me with no sympathy,
He lashed me with no pity
He lashed me with no empathy
He lashed me showing no mercy.

He left me bludgeoned and marred,
My face drowning in tears,
I strained to vanish him from my memory so hard,
As the sound of death filled my ears . . .

Rain

The rain clashes down on me,
Beating up my skin with its hard strokes.
It batters me, has me clutching my arms
Struggling to see through the enormous drops.
It cascades down bathing me till I'm cold,
Dropping me to my knees as it continues harshly.
So strong, while I'm so weak.
It consumes me, reminding me of my pain.
The raindrops are my tears

Nishka Dhawan

The end

What would you say, if I walked away
Would you let me leave, or stop me?
Would you finally open your eyes and see me?
Or would you treat me like you always have,
Leave me clinging to our lost friendship,
While I finally let go of your burden,
Finally live for someone other than you . . .
But with each day that passes,
Would you even miss me?
Wish you had behaved differently?
Or would you be happy,
Now that I left you alone!
Now that I'm gone!
Why did you never say anything?
Was it your ego, your anger?
Or was it something I deserved?
My pain, my agony, my tears
I drowned in for a year and a half,
You knew, I know, yet you left me alone,
Taught me I don't deserve you,
Or anyone else . . .
You gave me my place in life,
In your life . . .
You defeated me, you let me fall,
And I fell, I fell through time,
I fell till you taught me I was no one . . .
And no one was mine . . .

I never found out why.

I was in to day 5 of Kyle rejection. Five days back he told me it was over. Just that. It was my birthday and we were out on the ledge looking over the ocean. It was a perfect day. He made it perfect. The smell of the ocean wafted in the air and the breeze swayed my dark wavy hair to the side. I shivered slightly and he pulled me close wrapping his arm around me, his warmth emanating through my system. We stood like that for a while neither of us moving, just being content with holding each other. He broke the silence. "Sarah . . . I have something to say." I looked up though my lashes in to his beautiful green eyes. "What is it Kyle?" Casting his eyes down he looked away. "This is going to be harder than I thought" he said, sadness creeping in his tone. Now he had me worried. What was going on and why won't he look at me? "What's gonna be harder than you thought?" He sighed pulling me even closer to him, like that was possible. He buried his face in my hair inhaling deeply. The he kissed my head lingering for a while before letting go. In almost a whisper he said "saying goodbye." For a minute I thought I heard him wrong and I tilted my face up to look at him. His gorgeous face was bathed in melancholy. His eyes looking haunted. I had heard right. But why? "What did I do?"

"Nothing baby, I'm so sorry."

"Then why are you breaking up with me?" I said incredulous, tears burning the back of my eyes. He said nothing. "Kyle! Answer me" I screamed.

"Trust me it's for the best. It's for us." "How? What are you talking about? Leaving me? That's for the best? Kyle what's gotten in to you? Stop this . . . Please just stop this." I couldn't control it anymore. The tears started seeping from my eyes and once they began, they didn't stop. "I have to go now, it's time." He said as a farewell. Time for what? I didn't have the strength to say that. The next minute he was gone and it was just me hugging myself and crying my heart out. He was gone. He was actually gone. The next morning the news headline read, "Young teenager found dead last night." And it was him. He had left me forever and I never found out why . . .

I am nothing to him

He won't talk to me. It's weird though. Just a few years back we were the best of friends; I don't know what's happened now. When I look back in time tears fill my eyes as I can see me being happy. Him making me happy. And now, it's all over. Sometimes in the night I cry softly in to my pillow. I cry for what I have lost and for everything that has happened to me. In a sea of people I feel alone, misunderstood and when I see him if only for a fraction of a second I feel complete. But all to soon that moments over and he's gone and I'm lost again. It's time I need to sort things out. I can't stay away from him anymore, it's driving me crazy. When the school day finishes I quickly pack my belongings and head down early hoping to catch him before he leaves. I wait for a while sitting on one of the large brown chairs as I see him exit the stair case. I run after him hoping he gives me a minute. "Evan?" I call after him. He stops and I walk over to him. "What Natasha?" He sounds really annoyed and this hurts me. "What's going on with you? It's like we aren't even friends anymore, what did I do?"

"Nothing" that's it that's all he says and now I would've preferred if he lashed out at me. There's no emotion in his tone and I'm really starting to worry now. "Then what's wrong?"

"Nothing."

"Then why don't we talk anymore?"

"I don't talk much anymore, it's not just you."

Now I feel tears creeping in to my eyes. But I will not break down not in front of him. So I wasn't special anymore like he thought I was. Now I was just a 'someone' like everyone else in his life. Realization hit me so hard I almost stumbled. He didn't want me in his life,

I was nothing to him. I squeaked an "okay" out before exiting the school grounds in the opposite direction. The tears I had been holding back now fell endlessly. I am nothing to him.

SECTION 3

Hell:

"He was my North, my South, my East and West, My working week and Sunday rest, My noon, my midnight, my talk, my song; I thought that love would last forever: I was wrong."

—W. H. Auden

Sin

It can never be easy,
To watch him uncaring,
Or stay away when I'm hurting.
Life won't get better, just worse,
Just looking at him
    Is a sin.
For me, he may be poison,
But I look for him when I'm hurt.
He may be cruel, but he's my healer,
The guy who puts meaning to my life,
The guy I'd love no matter what they'd say.
Just talking to him
    Is a sin.
He may not care about me the way I do,
But I'd rather him hurt me than anyone else.
He doesn't belong to me, but I belong to him,
Even if he doesn't know that.
For I don't want anyone else, I want him.
Just loving him
    Is a sin.

Paradise

Cars zoom by,
    Time stops,
    The sun is setting,
The day is fading.
Paradise . . .
In the middle of the street.
Sounds consume me,
Blood everywhere,
Cries of his loved one,
Ringing through the despondent night.
The wailing sound of a siren,
Screams of everyone . . .
Watching
Waiting,
Weeping . . .
I stand resolute, as car zooms by.
Traffic lights flickering.
Paradise in the middle of the street.
Dark light, bright light,
Fill my eyes
But all I see is red
His blood . . . Everywhere.
And its paradise,
Paradise in the middle of the street . . .

Her dark beauty.

The night screamed out loud,
    As the wind whipped hard against the grass.
    All above the sky was a misty cloud,
The time slowed to a pause and wouldn't pass

600 years ago, he trotted across this land,
Hand with sword, body in gear.
Far across he saw her pale hand,
He swept towards her with a pang of fear.

Up close he saw her beauty in awe,
The slow movement of breathing in her chest.
Up above him a crow began to caw,
As he forgot his fear, watching her peacefully rest.

He knelt down beside her, love filling his eyes,
He stroked her cheek, in the blindning night.
Just then he felt the wind pick up and her arm rise,
As she gripped his neck, unwavering and tight.

Now the beauty vanquished from her features,
Her eyes flung open to reveal a fathomless black.
He realized she was no ordinary creature,
His muscles tightened awaiting an attack.

The pain hit fast, making his insides wail,
As she tore his flesh with maddening rage.
His blood swept across the road in a vicious trail,
She trapped him in her grasp as if she were a cage.

Slow and steady the pain simmered down.
He could gaze at the light right across the bridge.
He could feel himself in to death, drown,
As he made his way across the ridge.

Victory accomplished, her features morphed back to normal,
As she lifted herself and began to drift away.
The wind died and the night cleared off the paranormal,
As the night vanquished and the sun shone through the day.

But every 100 years she walks across this road,
Awaiting her next victim, in all her profound glory.
So as he strides across, the sky beginning to explode,
She gazes at him darkly and now we all know the story . . .

Satan's reincarnation

He strides along blending in to one of us,
But he's no god or son of Jesus.
He may fool you but he's far from fooling me,
Cause when I look in to his eyes this is what I see . . .

He's the life of darkness, the villain in every book,
The face of evil, the making of a crook.
Like the fallen angel who rebelled against god,
His every move is shady and flawed.

Burning like the fire he threatens whatever comes his way,
He takes away the light from each and every day.
Like the lion he treads ready to rip my flesh away,
He's the light of darkness, it's each and every ray.

Cold as a vampire who sucks the life out of me,
He blinds my eyes and drowns my thoughts in a sea.
Like a vicious snake whose poison runs in my veins,
He washes away my doubts of him, just like the rain.

He's the tumor controlling my brain,
The virus spreading through my veins,
A serial killer with creative ways,
He's as perplexing as a never ending maze.

Like the twister destroying everything with his lust,
He's the earthquake grinding me to dust.
Like the vicious dog with a mean bite,
He's the nightmare that haunts me all night.

He's the cage that holds me captive,
The reason why I don't want to live . . .
So I yearn for you to listen to me for
Dear god, he's not whom you believe him to be . . .

Fear

Light is the absence of dark,
Yet, fear lingers, leaving a mark.
Floods the mind with a gush of drear,
Clouds the vision making everything unclear.
Black, dark and cold it stays,
Controls and dominates ruining our days,
A sudden intuition to look behind our backs,
Wanting to always cover our tracks.
Hide, oh hide from the unknown it says,
You're not safe even in the sun's rays
It says . . .
Listen to fear, evil lurks out here.
We beg to disagree now and then,
But fear insists again and again,
Listen to me, oh listen to me,
It says . . .
Or you'll face the darkest of your days.
Dark it gives dark it takes,
Oh tell me how is this fair play?
Oh tell me, oh tell me what to do,
Oh, give me strength to breakthrough,
Tell me, oh tell me what is right,
Tell me, should I believe my sight?
Don't do this to yourself,
It says . . .
Beyond the light you cannot gaze,
Trust me, oh trust me I can,
Stay with me, oh stay with me,
You know you can . . .
You know you have to,
To save yourself you know what you have to do . . .

Stay with me, just stay with me,
There are things out there that only I can see,
Be with me, oh be with me,
Don't walk this earth so blindly,
Hold on to me, Oh hold on to me,
In darkness and light with you i'll always be . . .
I take your power away that's true,
But tell me, oh tell me what can I really do?
My job is to remind you of the evil out there,
To prepare you for the pain you'll have to bear,
So tell me, oh tell me, you're reason for keeping distance,
When all i'm doing is moulding your existence,
Making you in to a stronger you,
Giving you strength you never knew.
Once you conquer me forever,
No one can hurt you ever . . .
My strength lies in yours,
I give you keys to open new doors,
To become a new, stronger you,
Teach you more than you ever knew . . .
So stay with me, oh just stay with me,
It says . . .
There are things out there that only I can see,
Be with me, oh just be with me,
Don't walk this earth so blindly,
Hold on to me, just hold on to me,
In darkness and light with you i'll always be . . .

The sacrifice

Cowering, hiding amongst the darkness,
Petrified, bruised and hopeless,
Panicking thinking my end was near,
That he would soon find that I was here.
I wondered why I did it all,
When I knew in the end I would fall
Deep in to the depths of hell,
Forever, trapped in a diabolic cell.
I sold my soul ten years back,
When my loved one suffered a vicious attack,
And I didn't know what to do,
I hadn't the slightest clue.
Thats when I saw him,
Seeing him gave me a newfound vim,
He seemed godlike and celestial,
I couldn't believe that he was real.
He approached me with a wide grin,
Golden light glowed from his skin,
He asked me what was wrong,
And I told him my loved one wouldn't live long.
He came closer and looked in to my eyes,
Told me my loved one needn't die at sunrise,
If I gave up to him my soul,
And fell in to the deep hellhole.
I saw I didn't have a choice,
Ten years for me would have to suffice,
If I wanted my loved one back,
And I didn't think that "he" would make a comeback.
So he sealed the deal and disappeared,
Of him, I never feared,
Off course I was wrong,
Ten years weren't so long,

I began to fear that i'd see him again,
And that I'd be stuck in the devils den.
As the day neared I saw glimpses of him,
I was scared to stay alone when the lights went dim.
My loved one began to worry about me,
And I couldn't say what would become of me,
So I left home and ran away,
Cause it would be my end the next day.
I stopped when I reached a dead end,
How could I ever think he was godsend?
I wanted to save my soul,
Not fall in to the hellhole,
So I tried to hide amongst the darkness of the night,
Even though I knew i'd never see tomorrows light.
I sat steady and uniform,
And then in the distance I saw his form,
I knew there was no use hiding,
So I stood up trembling.
He looked the same as before.
The same striking blue eyes,
The same faint smile.
I knew there was no negotiating,
So I shut my eyes waiting.
He came close and held my throat,
My body sank away like a boat,
Soon I was taken to a deadly place,
My strangled heart began to race,
Here, the sky was blood red,
Every inch of land was covered by the dead,
Crying and praying for the all-mighty,
Little did they know,
That their prayers weren't even heard slightly.
Dark demons started to shut them up,
And put those poor souls in lock-up.
While I just stood there watching,
As the hell hounds began barking,

I tried to hide or find a safe place,
But soon I saw his face,
He moved closer as I stepped back,
Never had I met anyone with a soul that black,
He was near me in a mere second,
And there was no where for me to run,
He leaned in and spoke in to my ear,
" Welcome to hell,
Out here you'll be swell,
Live an eternity of pain
Where blood falls in the form of rain,
Eat the best of tortured souls,
Sleep in dreadful, molten holes,
Fight for survival against the demons
Pay for all your deadly sins,
Never will you see light,
For this is the land of night
Where you're darkest nightmares come true,
Where pain will seem like a blessing to you,
Because here we offer way more than that.
Here, fragrance is the scent of a dead rat,
One day in and you'll wish you were never born,
Each day you will spend wistful and forlorn.
Trust me, make the darkness you're friend,
Or poor girl you're life may never end.
But let me just say,
Do have a pleasant stay,
Because you are here for eternity,
No way in hell will you ever leave this city.
So relax, enjoy and have fun,
Because you're peaceful days are forever done."

Nishka Dhawan

I'm different

I see the light yet I feel the dark,
To every statement I add a question mark.
I feel the suns rays yet I know it's gonna rain,
Knowing which one is right,
I still choose the wrong lane . . .
I look beyond the truth,
Searching for wrong,
I look for things that don't belong.
I spend my days fearing tomorrow,
Always expecting pain or sorrow.
I stay awake when i'm asleep,
Tears don't fall from my eyes when I weep.
I stand when I want to run,
I can't do things that need to be done.
I believe it's night when I see the sun rise,
I can see your soul by looking in to your eyes.
I can tell in an instant if you're lying,
I can save someone from dying,
I can cause misery to those who hurt me,
I can change the course of destiny.
But this is not who I want to be,
I want to be normal like the people around me,
All I desire is for my powers to fade,
And not be the one I was made . . .

Untitled 10

White noise,
Streaming tears,
Heartache.
Screaming, praying, pleading.
"Let me out"
Save me, please.
Falling to your knees,
Head in hands,
Migraine.
You do this to me.

Torture

As emotions burst inside of me,
A gripping pain held my heart,
Without his love my soul would never be free,
Without him my insides were now cleaved apart.

I endured the torment while I could,
But I was crucified with abounding despair.
The agony washed out all my strength it could,
And the repentance and bereavement I could no more bear

Various emotions clasped my soul,
The atrocious arms of betrayal and loss tried to affix
themselves to my weary frame.
My heart bemoaned as it scalded to reveal a hole,
My physique aggrieved as it burst in to a fierce garnet flame.

I felt a twinge and let the torment deluge me,
As this impalement I could bear no more.
I let go of my resolve tearfully,
And shut my eyes, as my entity in to a million pieces tore.

Dark

Forlorn, I sat alone in the murk,
Around me ghostly figures began to lurk,
The air turned opaque and chilling,
Goose bumps all over me started springing,
Uncanny and blood curdling sounds startled me,
Everything around me turned obscure and eerie.
I felt spectral apparitions scrutinize my face,
Apprehensive and aghast I compelled myself to brace.
I sat unwavering and uniform,
Oblivious to the uproarious bedlam of the storm.
The clouds roared and the lightening began to crackle,
In the far distance I could distinctly hear the howl of a jackal.
Even though uneasy and strained I still sat resolute,
The convulsion in my limbs turned excruciating and acute.
I ultimately sucked up the courage to open my eyes,
But the night was calm to my surprise . . .

My hell

It's really hard to keep a straight face
Because when I see him my world flips over.
He makes my heart literally stop.
The butterflies fluttering around.
My mind can't make sentences.
My feet won't let me move.
For those few seconds I feel happy.
It's the only time I do though.
Once he's gone I'm back in hell.
My own personal hell.

Torn

Darkness devours my world,
I scream in pain and agony as I am hurled
Into the never ending pit of melancholy and distress,
The misery and torment I strive to suppress.
But the sorrow and grief linger on,
Somehow this profound anguish may never be gone.
A shadow of affliction encompasses my soul,
My ruptured spirit may never be whole.
In this muddle of dolor my mind lays ,
At my dysfunctional body my eyes gaze.
And under these interminable layers of woe and dejection,
Lies my mutilated heart wailing for affection.
Still here I am dismantled and despondent,
Struggling to live a life I shouldn't.

Reincarnation:

"I recognized you instantly. All of our lives flashed through my mind in a split second. I felt a pull so strongly towards you that I almost couldn't stop it."

— J. Sterling, In Dreams

Renegade angel

(Based on Adrian's description in A touch of crimson
by Sylvia day)

The late afternoon sun glints of his surreal wing
The dignity and loyalty, which he would carry to his grave,
The righteous sense of law, which he abides to,
The countless mortals whose lives he must save.
His followers by a million to him cling
As he is some mighty god or the creator himself.
His eyes, are the worlds eyes, have seen so much
The knowledge he has absorbed as the eons have passed,
His life lived by a guided book is such
That his demeanor shows no fault.
Emotions lay hidden deep beneath his soul
As no one may question his path, his role.
But the weather so subtlety gives him away
His feelings, no one better could ever say.
Rumbling clouds, his wrath of fury,
The "no nonsense" mood, that he must do his duty.
Moaning winds and steady rain,
The racing tumult of his sorrow.
While the morning dew, light of the sun,
His profound joy, his reason for existence.
Each day which goes by his immortal soul
Is strenuous, his mission his sight.
Protecting the mundane from the unnatural bloodsuckers
While the demons prowl in the depths of the night.
No love may be offered to him, for that is forbidden
And each day must be lived, without his rightful mate,
For if she was given to him, the creator dreads
He may alter his gait.

His eyes in a million hews of blue,
Sometimes cerulean, the color of the sea,
Sometime azure to blend into the night,
Each color as mesmerizing as the last
Shining brightly whether in darkness or in light.
As years go by, nothing will ever change,
His open wounds will still gush red.
His path to freedom, her soul
Still remains lost, her mortal body dead,
While he paces through dimensions abiding his role,
As alabaster wings, brighter than gold
Ruffle restlessly as time goes by,
And as each day passes no better than the last
All that remains is a forgotten past . . .

You did this.

The laughs that echoed through this room.
The smiles suppressed through biting lips.
Hidden conversations, day and night.
Just you. Just you.
Desolation , loneliness you took away.
Your sight made everything fade.
Late nights and early mornings
Nothing mattered when I was with you.
Just you. Just you.
Reality crashed, booming voices.
Tears, agony was all that remained.
The music faded. Screams echoed.
Ear piercing reality.
No more conversations,
No rest, no life.
Everything disappeared.
Because of you. Because of you.

Untitled 11

You're standing in front of me,
Holding my hands, pleading apologizing
And I forgive you.
Because I thought we were going to
Start over . . .
But did we?
Our past stands like a wall between us,
Our love lost, no trust.
Who are we fooling living like this?
When I can't even stand the
Sight of you . . .
When I can't even forget
How you betrayed me.
It was over a long time ago.

Your Return

How could you never know what I felt for you,
How could you ever let me leave
And say good-bye
Weren't you there when I said I love you,
My feelings exposed
While you said there was nothing you cloud do.
I left, oh how hard it was for me
And all you could say was " I'm sorry".
You never asked for me again
You took off in a different lane
We went our own separate ways
Never acknowledged each other
And so passed the days . . .
Rumors passed along
And so you heard
That I had met somebody
And u were outraged
You came back to me,
The fury shining in your eyes
While I wondered what was wrong
But you didn't say a word . . .
You came close and held me tight,
The world faded away
And everything seemed so right
When you touched your lips to mine
You made me shine
Brighter than diamonds . . .
Your kiss was sweet
The way two lovers for d first time meet,

But then it turned demanding
Asking questions I wasn't willing considering
I drowned in your kiss
Never had I felt such bliss . . .
Finally we broke apart
Your fury transformed to a new emotion,
Love, your love for me
A promise
A vow
A bond . . .

Untitled 12

Gone is the night of love
Like blood slowly draining out of you.
An empty bed, so cold, so vast and only you.
Outside you hear friendly chatter, a lover's meet
Like Romeo and Juliet that blissful romance
And the moon shines bright oh what a lovely night
Maybe to share a kiss or two
But here you are all alone.
Restless, hushing your tears.
Which keep flowing no matter your effort
And there's no one to comfort you
It's only you.
So you lie oh so restless,
Outside the wind blows a friendly tune.
Such a perfect night, so right
And here you are wretched and alone.
He never comes back it's only you . . .

Apologize

I committed a crime hard to express,
And now my soul cries in distress . . .
I pleaded for his forgiveness,
But his love for me had grown less . . .

He shoved me out of his door,
I felt low-spirited and heartsore . . .
Clutching my fists I banged on the wood,
From dusk to dawn outside his door I stood . . .
But he had locked the door to his heart,
And was determined to keep us apart . . .

He flushed out all our memories
Made his love for me cease,
While I drowned myself in agony and rue,
Pondering what else could I really do . . .

I tried one last time,
Hoping my sacrifice would make him forgive me of my
grievous crime . . .
I took in multiple stab wounds of grief and pain,
Hoping it would cleanse my soul of this dark stain,
I let myself succumb with guilt,
Like a rose beginning to wilt.
As I watched my surroundings engulf in darkness,
I saw a figure kneel beside me wailing for forgiveness,
Soon I realized it was him,
As the lights around me began to dim . . .
I wearily lifted my hand to touch his cheek,
But all to soon I started feeling weak,
My hand dropped to the ground with a thud,
I lay dead in a black pool of blood.

Untitled 13

You asked me to wait,
So I waited.
You asked me to trust you,
So I did.
But what did you do?
Lied to me. You cheated on me.
And I was so hopelessly in love with you!
I was waiting for you.
But you hurt me. You hurt me so much.
The pain I felt. The hatred.
And now you expect me to look past that.
Tell me how.
Tell me how should I love you,
When you made love to her.

It's over

You're standing in front of me,
I'm looking in to your eyes.
You're perfect in every way.
Your dark hair, wavy,
Those dark eyes searching mine,
Asking me questions,
But what can I say?
I know you can't be mine.
But I want you back.
We ended things I know,
You said it wasn't working out,
But I need you to know that I love you.
I love you so much
That it hurts seeing you here.
I can't stand you being so near me,
Looking in to my eyes,
Acting like you own me
Because you let me go
And I can't throw my arms around you.
I can't tell you I love you.
So we stand here, searching each other's eyes,
But we both know that it's over . . .

She's the one

She's standing in front of me,
Her eyes shining bright
And now I know
I made the right decision coming back.
God she looks beautiful,
Her dark hair fanning her face
And now I know
That she's the one.
I hate myself for the pain I put her through,
I can't forget her face when I told her
She fell apart, sobbing, begging
Me to not leave her.
But I still did.
And now I'm here
And she's here
And she says 'I do'
Nothing else matters now.
I'm forgiven.

Untitled 14

Time flies by, each day seems more tedious than the last.
Why won't he come back?
What did I do so harsh that about me he cares no more.
Or was it my downfall, ever believing he was mine.
He's still not here, so where is he?
The doorbell rings. I feel no heed to lift myself.
Ever since he left me this is my own private hell.
So I gingerly make my way to the door.
Wondering who's bothering my despair
And there he is standing in all his glorious beauty.
My heart melts at the sight of him.
My knees giving way.
The lump in my throat now bigger than ever
The tears getting harder to hold back.
"I'm sorry baby', He says.
And that's my undoing.
I fall in to his arms while he holds me steady.
"Please don't leave me again", I choke.
And we stand there for what feels like a lifetime
As silence descends over us, enveloping our love

A graduation present

I carefully wore my robes and brushed through my bedraggled hair hoping to pass as presentable. After half an hour of primping, I still looked horrid. Deep shadows hung down beneath my eyes, and my cracked lips burned as I tried again to heal them with extra lip balm. It was safe to say that no amount of grooming could change my current state. After sighing heavily at the girls reflection in the mirror, I walked down the stairs. My aunt saw me approach and smiled at me ruefully. Without a word, we exited the front door and drove to school in complete silence. As soon as we entered the auditorium for the graduation ceremony I saw his face. Sensing my presence he looked right at me, his eyes searching for answers to unasked questions. I gave him a half smile and stood by one of my classmates waiting for Mrs. Belmorth to begin her speech.

She started soon after, going on and on about the history of our school and our accomplishments. Then the awards ceremony began. Each student was called one by one to the massive wooden stage to receive their certificates. "Adrien Miller, university of Berkley scholarship recipient", Mrs. Belmorth announced. The crowd roared their applause and I had never been more proud of him. Just as he received his certificate, he looked straight at me and mouthed the three words that meant so much more than just that, "*I love you.*" "Ivy clyde", Mrs. Belmorth began, "proud recipient of the Juilliard scholarship, congratulations".

For one minute I couldn't comprehend what was happening, then Adrien came up beside me and nudged me forward to the stage, while whispering in my ear, "Told you so". I went up the stage, wondering whether this was a dream and I was yet to wake up to reality, but when i held the certificate and say my aunt beaming in the crowd, I knew this was no dream . . . I had made it in to Juilliard.

The one person I hoped to share this news with was my mum, and then reality hit me, she was gone . . . Amongst all the happy faces in the crowd i desperately wished one of them was hers. Incapable of tearing up in public, I accepted my certificate and left the stage and then the auditorium. I knew he had followed me and i didn't know whether to be grateful or annoyed. His last memory of me shouldn't be of me weeping for the past. I couldn't let him see me like this.

"Ivy", he slowly turned me to face him, bending his head to desperately look me in the eye. Looking down I refused to met his eyes. Slowly he tilted my chin up even after all my struggle to stop him from doing so. "Oh Ivy, don't do this, don't push me away, not now", he said desperation and rue creeping in his tone. I held my voice as steady as I could and tried to say what i came here to, "I can't . . ." but one look at him and I just couldn't, I knew I was being selfish, thinking only of myself and not what he deserved but right now . . . I desperately *needed* to be held by Adrien's arms.

As if he could read my mind, he extended his arms towards me and gathered me close. My head lay on his chest unmoving, while I tried to hold back the sobs desperately trying to escape my chest. We stayed in that position with him stroking my head for a few minutes, even though to me they felt like hours. Being there, held by his arms seemed safe, like nothing else mattered. My heart kept screaming at me that I belonged right there, with him, but my mind constantly reminded me of the truth. I had to let him go, he deserved better. I forced myself to blurt out the truth. "I can't be with you Adrien, I just can't."

He looked at me desperately, as if pleading with my eyes to take back the words i had just uttered. But I couldn't, I know he thought I was making a mistake, but I needed to heal, he *needed* to understand that. His death grip on my arms never wavered though. He held me there, looking in to my eyes, as if hoping this was a bad dream. After a long stretch of silence he finally said, *"Why* Ivy, *Why"*. The desperation in his tone made me cringe, but he needed to know. Tight lipped i said, "Because you deserve better and because I need time." "Then let me wait for you ivy, don't push me away!" He said almost angry. " I *can't* make you do that Adrien, what if i'm too broken? What if I never recover from this? You'd regret it later, being with me! I'm saving you the regret, don't you see?" It took all my resolve not to tear up at this moment. He finally let go off my hands and I thought he'd finally understood my point. Instead, he locked his hands on my waist and bought his lips passionately to mine.

He kissed my lips with fervor, as if I was his anchor, his lips melded against mine as they fitted like two pieces of a broken heart, and, just like that Adrien healed me. His lips never leaving mine, prodded me to give in to him. To take back every word I said, and for a moment i couldn't even remember i was supposed to end things with him. As he savored me, his kissed turning demanding, i felt my knees give in, and just like that he lifted me up with ease. His one hand now rested at the back of my thigh, while his other hand cupped the back of my head. I held on to him for dear life, knowing that he *owned* me now. His connection to me just grew stronger. As he tasted my lips again and again, I realized that I was a part of him and no matter how much i'd make him wait, or push him away, he'd *always* come back to me. Always.

His unsaid confession made me shudder. He probably noticed it as he immediately parted his lips from mine, but still held me suspended mid air. I couldn't even care if anyone saw us like this, it just felt so right. "Talk to me

Ivy, tell me what's on your mind." I looked straight in to his eyes as I answered. "You, Adrien. You're on my mind and you wont leave. I was supposed to break up with you today . . ." I trailed off. "Well are you breaking up with me today?" He said. His voice had turned somewhat cold and he lowered me to the ground. Once i stood upright I replied in a single breath, " how can I? How can you even expect me to think straight when you kiss me like that? I feel selfish not being able to go through with it, horrible even cause you deserve better and I am not better but what can I say Adrien? I'm unconditionally and irrevocably in love with you" "*Ivy* . . . I love you too, you know that, you also know that there's no one else I'd rather be with. So if you are broken, let me fix you. If you need time, let me wait. But if you think I deserve better, then you obviously don't realize just how much you mean to me . . . You're my everything ivy, and so much more"

His confession seeped through me, filling every ounce of my frame with his love for me. It flooded my veins, seeped through my blood and enraptured my heart, claiming it. He would *never* let me go, and that thought overwhelmed me.

Farewell

My journey seems short,
Unopened chapters of life still left unsaid.
A million thoughts, a million shades
Which I wished to share.
Those never ending thoughts so hard to frame,
So difficult to put on a page,
Yet here I am at the end
Wishing you farewell
Away from this fictional land.
We part ways now
But I thank you for joining me
On this journey.
But you and I both know
That the journey of love is a never-ending one.
Its twisted paths and destinations
All muddle up to form one complicated maze.
You leave me now, this book behind
But you take away the truth of love,
Harsh yet so sweet,
Love is a man's treasure.